TURTLE RESCUE!

adapted by J-P Chanda
based on the original teleplay by Eric Luke
illustrated by Jesus Redondo

Ready-to-Read

Simon Spotlight

New York   London   Toronto   Sydney

Based on the TV series *Teenage Mutant Ninja Turtles*™
as seen on Fox and Cartoon Network™.

SIMON SPOTLIGHT
An imprint of Simon & Schuster Children's Publishing Division
1230 Avenue of the Americas, New York, New York 10020

Manufactured in the United States of America

First Edition

2 4 6 8 10 9 7 5 3 1

Library of Congress Cataloging-in-Publication Data
Chanda, J-P.
Turtle rescue! / adapted by J-P Chanda ; based on the original teleplay by Eric
Luke; illustrated by Jesus Redondo.— 1st ed.
p. cm. — (Ready-to-read)
Summary: April learns how the turtles became ninjas and enlists their help
against the bank-robbing Mousers of Dr. Stockman.
ISBN 0-689-87007-8 (pbk.)
[1. Turtles—Fiction. 2. Heroes—Fiction. 3. Martial arts—Fiction.] I. Redondo,
Jesus, ill. II. Teenage Mutant Ninja Turtles (Television program) III. Title.
IV. Series.
PZ7.C35927 Tu 2004
[Fic]—dc22
2003019180

April O'Neil had a weird dream:
Mouser robots were chasing her
through the sewers. Then she was
saved by giant **turtles**!
She was glad it was only a dream.

"Hi," said Leonardo.

"Hey there!" Raphael said.

April stared in shock.

She hadn't been dreaming at all.

"Where am I?" she finally asked.

"At our pad," Donatello said.

"We saved you," added Leonardo.

Just then Master Splinter came in.

"You **can't** be real!" April said.

"Young lady, I promise we are very real," said Splinter. "And we need your help."

"But how can you talk—?" April asked.

Master Splinter sat quietly

for a moment.

"Listen," he began, "and

I will tell you our story."

"It was a day that started
like any other—until I saw a
blind man crossing the road.
A truck was headed straight for
him. On the opposite curb stood
a boy, who was carrying a jar
of four young turtles.

"At the last minute the boy
pushed the blind man
out of the way. The truck turned,
and a strange can fell out.

"The boy dropped the jar into the sewer. The can also fell into the sewer. It smashed open and covered the four turtles with a glowing ooze.

"I brought the turtles home.

I cleaned off the ooze,

getting some on myself.

"The next day I saw that the turtles had doubled in size. I was changing too. It must have been the ooze!

"The turtles grew.

They learned to walk and speak.

I trained them to become ninjas.

"I chose their names—
Leonardo, Donatello, Raphael, and
Michelangelo—from an art book
I found.

"They became the

TEENAGE MUTANT NINJA TURTLES!"

When his master's story ended, Raphael asked April, "Why were those Mousers chasing **you**?"

"My boss, Dr. Stockman, built the Mousers," April said. "When I found out he was using them to rob banks, he sent them after me."

Michelangelo pointed to the screens.

"Guys, they are at it again!" he yelled.

"We have to stop them," said Raphael.

"I know where Stockman's lab is," said April. "I can help."

"Oh, yeah!" cheered Michelangelo.

"It's Mouser-smashing time!"

April led the Turtles through the sewers to Stockman's lab. When they were close she stopped them and said, "Careful. Video cameras."

They climbed through an air shaft.

Then the Turtles silently slipped into

the shadows and headed for the lab.

These guys are good, April thought.

"Wow! Anybody want to buy a
Mouser?" Michelangelo joked
when they entered the lab.
Just then a voice boomed from above.
"Intruders! Strange-looking ones!"
"It's Dr. Stockman!" April cried.

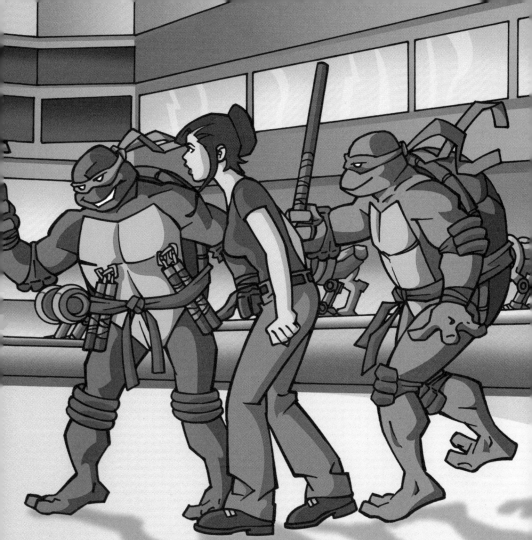

"April, you're alive!" Dr. Stockman said.

"But not for long."

He pressed a button and

the lasers took aim.

"Not good," Michelangelo said

with a gulp.

The lasers fired! April jumped out
of the way and the Turtles sprang
into action. They blocked. They sliced.
They diced. They SMASHED!

Finally Leonardo shouted, "It's over!"

"That's what you think," Dr. Stockman replied, as he pressed another button. Mousers began to swarm in from all directions.

Donatello and April rushed to
the control panels while the others
fought off the Mousers.

But there were too many of them.

The Mousers closed in.

"Game over, guys!" cried Raphael.

April typed one last thing into the keyboard. And the Mousers froze! "You did it!" the Turtles cheered. "**We** did it," said April. "Let's get out of here before they explode."

April and the Turtles rushed out
of the lab with the Mousers exploding
behind them. They jumped
into the sewer in the nick of time.

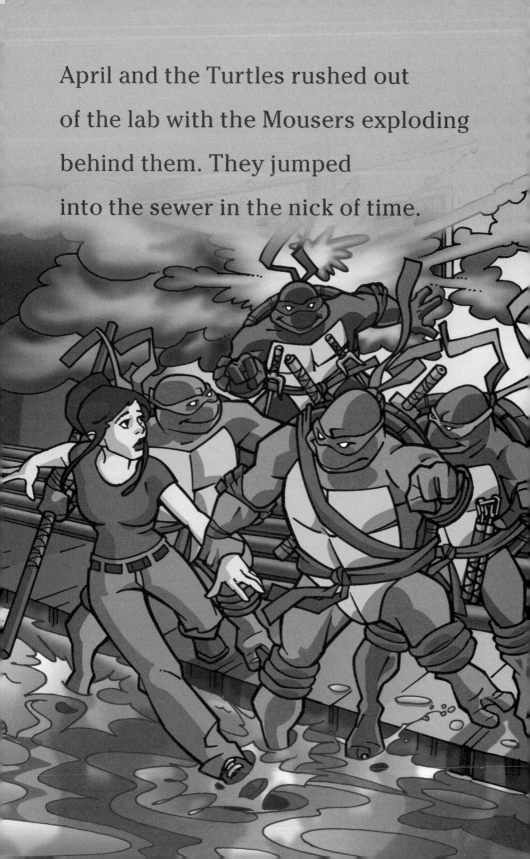

Later that night the Turtles

welcomed their new team member.

"Here's to April!" they cheered.

"You must promise to keep our

secret," Splinter told April.

"I will," April said, smiling.

"Besides, who would believe me if I told them?"